Safety and
people who help us

Peter G Aid

NIGEL SNELL

Hamish Hamilton · London

All his life Peter had found
it hard to hear people.

He couldn't hear his tortoise,
and I'm not sure his tortoise
could hear him!

He could hardly hear his mother (which was lucky sometimes when he was naughty).

And he couldn't hear his teacher.
She used to get rather cross!

And because he couldn't hear himself, Peter spoke in a funny way. His friends laughed at him and Peter was sad.

When he was little, Peter had been to an ear doctor. Now his mummy was taking him to see the doctor again.

One fine day they left the house and drove to the town.

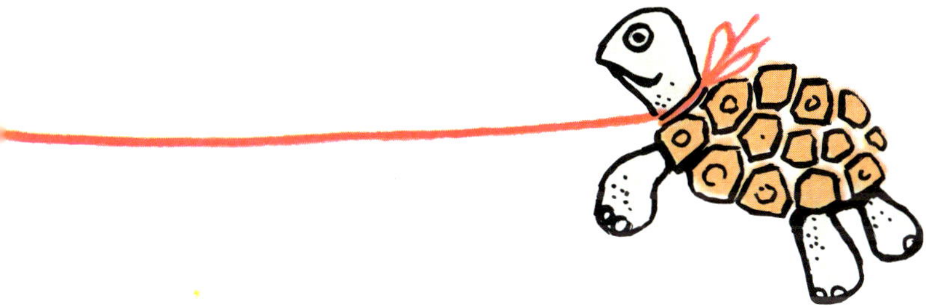

Peter's tortoise was very excited. He hadn't been there before!

They arrived at the hospital
and went into the waiting room.
There were lots and lots of other
boys and girls. But Peter's
tortoise had to stay in the car.

The doctor took Peter into a tiny room. There were drums, zylophones and rattles on a shelf, but the doctor said that they were only used to test babies' hearing. She looked into Peter's mouth.

Then she looked in Peter's ears
with a kind of torch.
It was rather cold and it tickled!

The doctor put headphones on Peter. They went Buzzzzz and Pinggggg as the doctor twiddled the knobs.

Peter pretended
he was a pilot!

“We must get you a new hearing aid”, said the doctor.

She pressed some rubbery stuff into Peter’s ear to make an ear mould. It would fit his ear exactly.

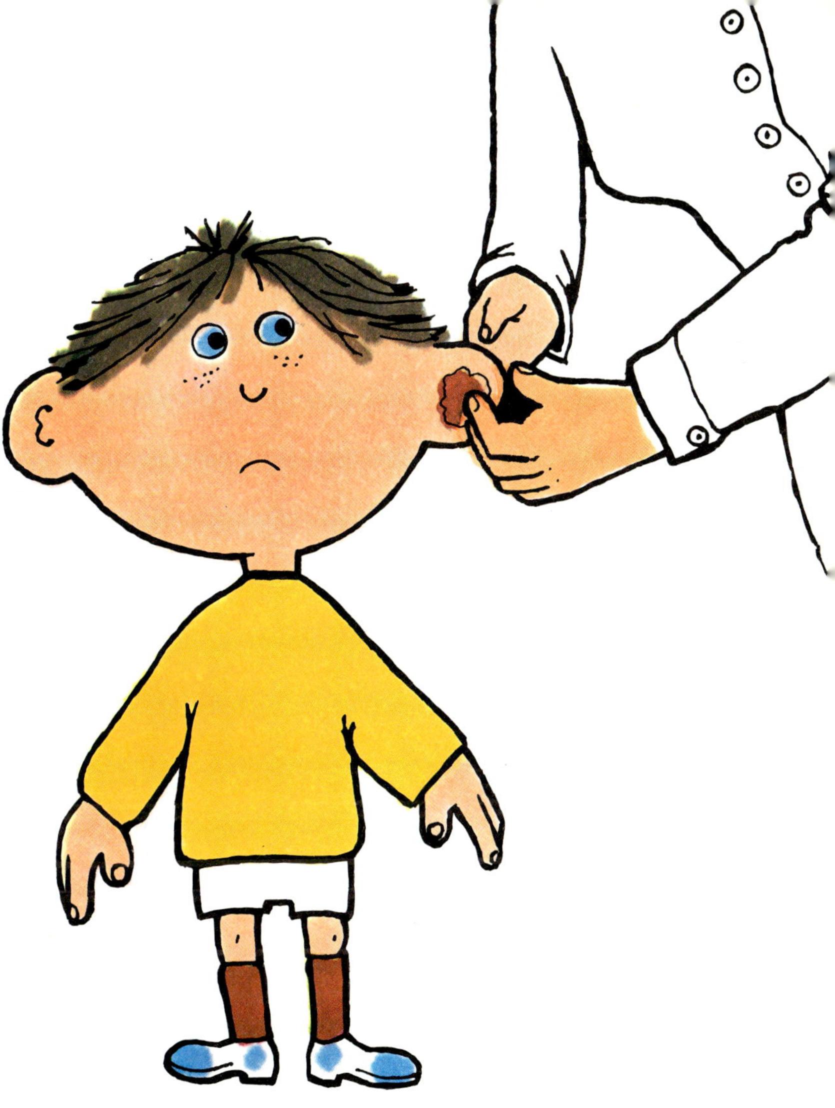

When Peter next
came to the hospital,
he was given a
tiny hearing aid.

It went behind his ear.
A small plastic tube joined it
to the mould in his ear.
No-one noticed it, but
Peter could hear much better.

He could hear his Mum.

And his Dad.

And his teacher . . .

and buses . . .

and birds . . .

. . . but his tortoise didn't say much. He just smiled.
And so did Peter.